This book belongs to

Mary

GEORGIE and the NOISY GHOST

by Robert Bright

SCHOLASTIC BOOK SERVICES
NEW YORK • TORONTO • LONDON • AUCKLAND • SYDNEY • TOKYO

ISBN: 0-590-09347-9

14 13 12 11 10 9 8 7 01/8

Printed in the U.S.A.

07

For Anthony

Now a proper house has just one ghost and the ghost who lived in the Whittaker's house was Georgie. Georgie was so little, he was so gentle, he never more than creaked the stairs and squeaked the parlor door, and that was just right.

But one summer Mr. and Mrs. Whittaker rented a house on the beach for the holidays. Everybody came along—Herman the cat, Miss Oliver the owl

and Georgie of course.
They arrived at sunset.

First thing Miss Oliver found a handy tree for herself and Georgie explored his nice new attic. It was so cluttered with wonderful old things it was just like home.

Downstairs Herman made friends with a mouse who lived behind a grandfather clock and they both watched Mr. and Mrs. Whittaker take out the little boat that came with the house.

Mr. and Mrs. Whittaker had such a good time rowing around, Miss Oliver had to fly out and hoot to remind them how late it was.

Then they went to bed and to sleep just as usual and the grandfather clock struck ten. After that it struck eleven and there was nothing wrong with that.

But when that grandfather clock struck twelve times somebody came up the cellar stairs and opened the cellar door.

He wore big boots that thumped and a big sword that rattled.

He marched straight to the front stoop and howled. He HOWLED! He howled seven times before he marched back down into the cellar.

Upstairs Mr. and Mrs. Whittaker woke up with a start. They thought it was the wind that was howling and pulled the covers over their heads.

But Georgie and his friends knew there was another ghost in the house, and he looked to be the noisiest and scariest ghost they had ever seen.

But the mouse, who knew all about him, said that he wasn't scary at all. He was just noisy because he was unhappy. His name was Captain Hooper and he had sailed the stormy seas in his time. But although he was a good captain, he had never managed to be a hero. So nobody—nobody—had ever given him a medal.

That's why he gloomed in the gloomy cellar and thumped and rattled and howled every night at twelve. He wanted everybody to know how unhappy he was. And he wasn't about to stop until somebody gave him a medal.

But how could anybody give a medal to a big noisy ghost who woke up the Whittakers way past bedtime?

Just the same Georgie knew something had to be done about it. He and Herman ransacked the attic until they found slippers and a nightshirt.

They left them in the cellar while the captain slept. But his boots and sword they hid away so he couldn't find them again.

Now that was good, because next night
Captain Hooper didn't thump any more
and he didn't rattle any more. BUT!!!!

He still howled at the sea because he didn't have a medal.

And that was bad. Because Mr. and Mrs. Whittaker woke up again with a start. This time they thought it was a hound-dog howling at the moon, and they jumped right out of bed.

They looked all over everywhere and were so upset they couldn't get to sleep again and sat up in the parlor for the rest of the night.

Next morning they were so tired they yawned all day long.

And when they took out the boat for a refreshing ride in the cool of the evening, they fell fast asleep. That was a fine how-do-you-do!

It was a good thing Herman was watching. Because that little boat drifted way out to sea.

Then black clouds came up and a thick fog came down and it grew as dark as pitch.

Herman gave the alarm to Georgie and Miss Oliver and they went up and down the beach meowing and hooting to beat the band. But Georgie knew that wasn't nearly noisy enough to save the Whittakers.

There was just one person noisy enough for that. They'd have to wake up Captain Hooper right away—before it was too late.

Now Herman meowed but that didn't wake the captain. Miss Oliver hooted but that didn't wake him.

But Georgie fetched a frying pan and a big spoon. Georgie beat that pan twelve times with the spoon. And that woke up Captain Hooper.

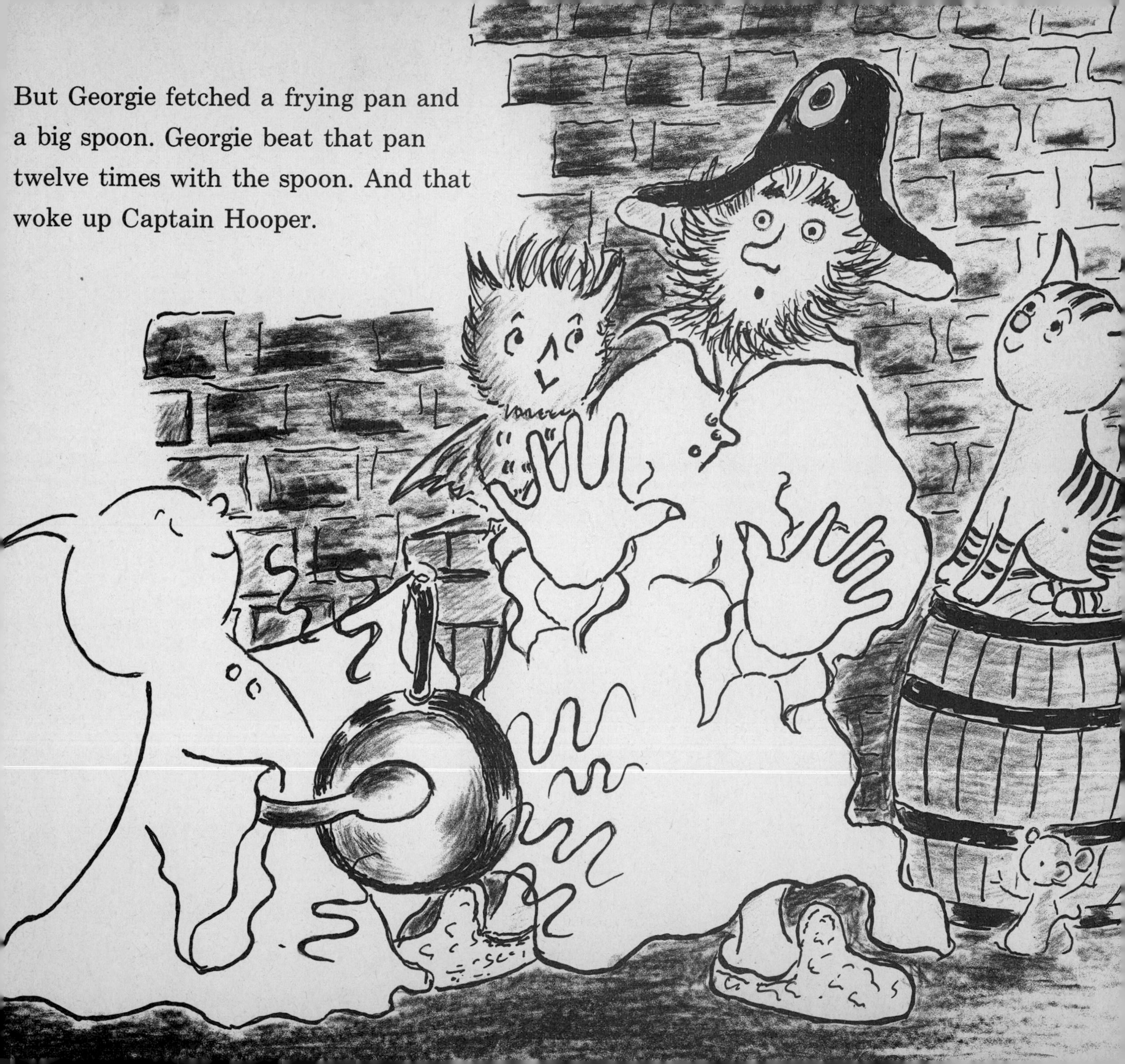

They told him that Mr. and Mrs. Whittaker were lost in a boat at se and that only he could save them. But he would have to howl louder and longer than he had ever howle before.

That's just what Captain Hooper did.

Far out at sea Mr. and Mrs. Whittaker woke up with a start. And what a surprise to find they weren't home in bed! But they weren't scared because they heard the familiar sound that had waked them.

This time they knew it wasn't the wind and it wasn't a hound-dog. So they decided it must be a friendly foghorn and Mr. Whittaker knew exactly which way to row.

Now Captain Hooper wasn't a foghorn. But he was louder. And he was a hero because he saved the Whittakers.

Up in the attic, later on, Georgie himself gave Captain Hooper a medal. And everybody cheered.

Captain Hooper was so happy he never howled again. He stayed in the cozy attic and went haunting with Georgie every night.

Georgie taught the captain how to creak the stairs and squeak the parlor door.

One night he let him do it all by himself.

Captain Hooper haunted so gently
and Georgie was so proud of him, h
just had to give him another medal

Thank goodness!